WHEN THE WORLD BEGAN

Stories collected in Ethiopia

ELIZABETH LAIRD

Illustrated by
Yosef Kebede, Emma Harding,
Grizelda Holderness, and Lydia Monks

OXFORD
UNIVERSITY PRESS

Contents

When the World Began

When the world began, and God had created Man and all the animals, he called them to him and said, 'Tomorrow, when the cock crows, come to me and I'll give you your gifts.'

Now the Buffalo was God's favourite animal. He loved him better than all the others.

'Come early,' God whispered in the Buffalo's ear. 'When you see the morning star rise in the sky, come to me then and I'll give you the best gift of all.'

The Dog overheard. He ran at once to the Man.

'Listen,' he said. 'The first creature to come to God will get the best

5

gift of all. Get up early. Don't wait for the cock to crow or the morning star to rise. Run to God as soon as you wake up.'

So before the cock had crowed, when the morning star had just lifted itself above the horizon, the Man ran to God. He had disguised himself with a buffalo skin and God did not recognize him.

'Who are you?' God called.

'I am the Buffalo,' answered the Man, 'and I've come for my gift.'

'You are the first, and the one I love most,' said God, 'and the best gift of all is for you,' and he gave the Man a spear.

Then the Buffalo arrived.

'Who is that, coming now?' said God.

'I am the Buffalo,' the Buffalo said. 'Don't you know me?'

'But you came earlier,' God said, 'and I gave you the best gift of all.'

'I didn't come,' said the Buffalo. 'That was the man. He tricked you.'

And the Buffalo roared with anguish.

God was sad.

'I wanted to give the best gift to you,' he said to the Buffalo, 'but the Man deceived me and I gave it to him. Now all I have for you is horns.'

So he gave the Buffalo horns, and the Buffalo and all the other cattle have worn them to this day.

But because the Man had the spear, he became the Buffalo's master, and the master of all the cattle, and they became his servants for ever more.

How the Tortoise Got Her Shell

When God first made the Tortoise, she had no shell.
She was naked, like the Lizard or the Frog. But the
Tortoise couldn't run fast like the Lizard and she
couldn't jump like the Frog. She was weak.

The other animals saw how weak the Tortoise was. One day, when they were all together in the deep, dark forest, they began to talk about her.

'She's a plump, tasty-looking thing, that Tortoise,' said the Lion.

'Yes,' agreed the Leopard. 'She looks juicy and good to eat.'

'She doesn't have any poison, like me,' said the Snake.

'Or sharp teeth, like me,' said the Crocodile.

'Or talons, like me,' said the Eagle.

'And the best thing of all,' the Hyena pointed out, 'is that she doesn't have any relatives. Who would stand up and fight for her?'

'You're right,' the Vulture nodded. 'She hasn't got any friends, either.'

'Wait a minute,' said the Lion, turning to the Skyhawk. 'I thought you were the Tortoise's friend?'

The Skyhawk fluttered his wings nervously and hopped from one foot to another.

'Who? Me?' he squawked. 'No, I'm not the Tortoise's friend. Whatever gave you that idea?'

'Then we're all agreed,' said the Lion. 'Tomorrow, when the sun is high, we'll meet again, and we'll find the Tortoise and tear her to pieces. We'll share out the meat between us all.'

None of the animals noticed the Mouse. She had scampered away, and was running through the forest, her little heart pumping inside her tiny chest. She ran all through the night, and when the morning came, she arrived at the place where the Tortoise was sunning herself on a rock.

'Dear Tortoise!' she panted. 'At last I've found you! Listen. There's going to be a terrible catastrophe. All the animals have joined together against you. They're coming to hunt you today. They're going to kill you and tear you to pieces and share out your flesh between them.'

'What?' gasped the Tortoise. 'They're coming to kill me? They're going to eat me?'

'Yes,' said the Mouse.

'Who thought of this?' asked the Tortoise. 'Which of the animals was there?'

'All of them,' answered the Mouse. 'The Lion, the Leopard, the Snake, the Crocodile . . .'

'Didn't the Eagle stand up for me?'

'No.'

'Didn't the Baboon say anything?'

'No.'

'And the Skyhawk? I'm sure he took my part.'

But the Mouse just shook her head.

'What?' wept the Tortoise. 'The Skyhawk wants to eat me too? I thought he was my friend!'

The Mouse said nothing. She was too upset. And the Tortoise began to sob.

'Who'll help me? Who'll save me?' she cried. 'I don't have any friends. I'm not very strong and I can't run fast. I don't have sharp teeth or claws. Mouse, dear Mouse, let me ask you one more thing. Was God there? Did he join in with all the others?'

The Mouse thought for a moment. Then she shook her head.

'No,' she said. 'I don't think God was there. I didn't see him, anyway.'

'Then,' said the Tortoise, 'I still have a chance,' and she began to pray.

The sun was climbing up and up and soon it was high in the sky. The animals had all met again, and they set off to hunt for the Tortoise. It had taken all night for the Mouse, running as fast as she could, to come to where the Tortoise lived, but the other animals galloped there fast on their big, long legs, and the birds flew even faster on their broad wings.

'I'm sure she lives around here somewhere,' said the Hyena, standing on a strange, new, round stone, just by the very rock where the Tortoise had been sunning herself that morning.

'I saw her here only yesterday as I flew overhead,' agreed the Eagle.

'We must hunt, hunt, hunt,' roared the Lion, and the animals ran round searching for the Tortoise, getting hotter and thirstier in the blistering sun.

At last they were too exhausted to go on any longer and they gave up hunting and slunk away into the forest, tired and hungry.

The strange, new, round rock moved, and the Tortoise poked her head out from inside it. Her friend, the Mouse, ran out from underneath.

'He saved me! God saved me!' cried the Tortoise. 'Now I know I'll be safe from all my enemies.'

'Yes,' said the Mouse. 'And we know something else, too. We know that God looks after the weak just as much as he looks after the strong.'

The Best Home

An old man who had two sons called them to him
one day and said, 'My dear sons, I'm getting old now
and I want to see you happily settled before I die.
Go out now and each of you build a home. Then come
back when a month has passed and tell me
how you have succeeded.'

So the two sons hurried away to make homes for themselves.

The first son went to the forest and cut down some fine tall trees. Then he carried them on his back to a beautiful site near the river and began to build himself a group of splendid huts.

'Well, brother,' he said to the younger son. 'Have you cut trees yet to make the framework of your huts?'

'No,' said his brother. 'I've been visiting my friend. His family have been very kind to me. They tell me I'm like a son to them and that I can stay with them whenever I like.'

'You're a fool,' the older brother said, and he cut laths for the walls of his huts and mixed straw and mud to cover them. Everyone could see what fine huts they would be.

'Now, brother,' he said to the younger son. 'Have you cut the laths and mixed the straw and mud to build the walls of your huts?'

'Oh no,' his brother answered. 'I've been visiting another friend. We've become blood brothers and have exchanged vows of eternal friendship. I can eat at his house whenever I'm hungry.'

'How stupid you are!' his older brother said, and he hurried off to fetch straw to make high smooth roofs to his huts.

When he had finished making the roofs, he said to his brother, 'So, brother, have you cut the straw yet to make the thatch for your huts?'

'Not yet,' his brother said. 'Another family has made me their closest friend, as if I was their adopted son. They beg me to spend my time with them whenever I can.'

When a month had passed, the two brothers went home to see their father.

'Now, my sons,' the old man said, 'take me to see your homes.'

The eldest son, filled with pride, took his father to see his fine new home. They stepped into the compound through the new fence of thorns and the father looked around admiringly. He walked to the first hut and said to his son, 'Is anyone here in this hut? Will anyone come out and offer us food?'

'No,' his son answered. 'No one's here.'

The old man walked to the second hut.

'Hello,' he called out. 'Is anyone there, to bring us out some water?'

No one answered. No one was there.

The old man walked on to the third hut.

'This is the finest and biggest hut of all,' he said to his son. 'Is there no one in this one, who can bring out a cowskin for us to sit on?'

'No, the hut's empty,' his oldest son said.

'I'm tired,' the old man said, 'and I'm hungry and thirsty. Let's go home.'

The next day he said to his younger son, 'Take us to see your home.'

The younger son took his father and brother to the first family he had befriended. They welcomed them with open arms and gave a big feast for them, offering them more food than they could possibly eat.

Then they went to the second family who had taken him in as if he had been their own son. They slaughtered a sheep and plied them with food and drink until the sun went down.

On they went to the third family who had taken the younger son to their hearts. They killed a cow in his honour and entertained their three guests as if they were princes.

The old man set off for home, replete with good things.

He turned to his first son and said, 'You did well, my son, to build yourself such fine huts, but they are sad and cold and empty. They are not a real home.'

Then he looked at his younger son. 'You have done better,' he said. 'You have found love and warmth and friendship. That's what a true home should be, and you'll reap its benefits for the rest of your life.'

Nyap and Nyakway

Once upon a time there were two girls called Nyap and Nyakway. They were sisters, and they lived with their parents in a hut in the shade of a huge old mango tree, deep in the forest of Gambella.

Nyap was a beautiful girl, but she was spoiled and vain. When she went to the river she would never bring water back for her mother, or help her father with the fish. She would simply stand at the brink, admiring her reflection in the still water of the pool by the bank. She spent nearly all her days at home, lying on a cowskin outside the hut, playing with the beads she wore round her neck and admiring her own elegant long legs.

'Come here!' she would call out to Nyakway, her sister. 'I'm hungry. Bring me a ripe mango. I'm thirsty. Get me something to drink.'

The girls' parents loved Nyap. They never made her do any work.

They never made her pound grain, or sent her out to look after the cattle, or asked her to sweep the dead leaves away from the door of the hut.

It was Nyakway who did all the work.

'You useless creature!' her mother would screech. 'Why don't you go and help your father to bring home his catch?'

'Lazy girl,' her father would shout when he came home from fishing in the river. 'Why isn't my food ready?'

One day, when their father came home with a bigger haul of fish than usual, his wife said, 'Where am I going to clean all this fish? I need something to put them on.'

Nyap was lolling against the trunk of the mango tree.

'Make Nyakway lie down,' she said. 'Use her back. She's no good for anything else.'

'Oh, my darling,' said her mother. 'How clever you are! What a good idea. Come here, you stupid Nyakway. Lie down and don't you dare move.'

So poor Nyakway lay down in the dust and her mother used her back as a table while she cleaned and cut the fish. But Nyakway bore it all without a murmur.

Nyap and Nyakway had an older sister who had been married to an ogre many years before, and who lived far away through the deep dark forest. One day, she sent a message to her parents, asking for one of her sisters to visit her.

'I'm not going,' said Nyap. 'Walk alone for miles and miles through the deep dark forest? Stay with an ogre? Not me.'

'Of course you mustn't go, my precious,' said her mother. 'Supposing a leopard jumped out on you, or you trod on a snake, or you lost your way? I'd be so worried about you I wouldn't have a moment's peace. Nyakway can go. We can quite easily do without her.'

So Nyakway set off through the deep dark forest. She carried a little food in her hand, which was all her mother would spare her, and her heart beat fast with excitement and fear. The path was long and winding. Once she heard a lion roaring in the distance. Once she passed a python coiled up waiting, under a tree. But she walked on and on. When evening came, she smelled the smoke of her sister's fire and followed it to her hut.

Her sister was very pleased to see her and so were her nephews and nieces who tugged at their aunt's hand, climbed into her lap and showed her all their little games.

Soon, the ogre, her brother-in-law, came home from hunting. Nyakway greeted him respectfully and helped her sister to prepare his food. His teeth were long and his eyes were round, but he smiled at her kindly and made her welcome.

The days passed quickly at her sister's house. Nyakway helped to fetch the water and pound the grain. She looked after the children and swept the dead leaves away from the door of the hut, just as she had always done at home. Weeks passed, and then months. Nyakway was very happy. Her sister's family loved her, and she loved them too.

But one morning, Nyakway woke up and knew that it was time to go home. Everyone was sad to see her go. The children clung to her knees and asked her for one last story. Her sister made her a breakfast of delicious food to keep her satisfied all day long. Only her brother-in-law the ogre didn't come to say goodbye. He was nowhere to be seen.

Nyakway set off. The path was long and winding. She heard strange rustling noises in the trees overhead, but when she looked up, she could only see a big white bird. She didn't know that her brother-in-law had changed himself into an eagle and was flying overhead. She heard sticks snapping in the undergrowth near the path, but when she looked round she could only see the hind legs of an animal, bounding away between the trees. She didn't realize that her brother-in-law had changed himself into a bushbuck and was running on ahead of her.

Suddenly, she stopped. There, right in front of her, was the most beautiful tree she had ever seen in her life. Huge, juicy fruits hung down from its branches, its leaves glittered like gold, and a delicious smell wafted from it, making her head spin.

'Nyakway! Nyakway!' said the tree. 'Come here and eat my fruit!'

Nyakway put out her hand to touch the tree, but then she remembered the breakfast her kind sister had made for her.

'Thank you very much,' she said, 'but I'm not hungry just now. I've been with my dear sister, who made a special meal for me, and my heart is full of sadness at leaving behind her kind, good family. I couldn't eat a thing.'

Gently, she pushed the branches aside and walked on. The tree changed back at once into the ogre, who bounded on invisibly ahead of her.

Nyakway walked and walked. It was late now and the sun was sinking in the sky. Her heart was sinking too. She didn't expect to be welcomed home.

Suddenly she stopped. There, on the path ahead of her, was a wonderful dish of dried fish, dripping with butter, with a fine spoon ready and waiting beside it.

'Nyakway! Nyakway!' the dish called out. 'Aren't you hungry? Why don't you eat? I'm so delicious, you'll never have anything so good for the rest of your life.'

Nyakway reached down and touched the spoon. But then she thought of the kind sister she had left behind and the cruel one she was going back to, and she didn't feel hungry any more.

'Thank you,' she said. 'I'm sure you're very good to eat, and I'm grateful to you for asking me, but I'm not hungry. I've left my dear sister and her good husband and children, and I'm too sad to eat.'

Carefully, she stepped over the dish and went on her way.

The dish immediately disappeared and the ogre stood in its place. At once he turned into a leopard and ran back through the forest to his home.

Nyakway arrived at her father's house tired and hungry. Her parents were pleased to see her.

'I'm tired of fetching water myself all the time,' said her mother, 'and your sister never helps me. I'm glad you've come home at last.'

'No one's helped me to carry my fish back from the river since you went away,' her father said. 'It's a good thing you've come back.'

'Oh, there you are,' yawned Nyap. 'Come here and plait my hair.'

Things went on as before, but Nyakway was happier. She still did all the work, and Nyap still did nothing, but her parents were kinder to her now. They'd missed her while she'd been away.

Nyakway liked to talk about her sister's hut and her sister's family, and Nyap liked to listen. One day, Nyap said, 'I want to go and visit our sister. It's obviously much nicer there than in this boring place.'

Her parents tried to persuade her not to go, but she'd made up her mind, so off she went. Her mother prepared a big bundle of delicious things for her to eat on the journey, and her father walked with her nearly all the way. Once they heard a lion roaring in the distance.

'It won't come near us,' her father said.

Later, they saw a python lying coiled near a tree.

'Wait here while I kill it,' her father said.

Nyap came at last to her sister's house. She was tired and hungry. Her sister was very pleased to see her, and her nephews and nieces hung around her, trying to climb into her lap and tell her all their little secrets. But she slapped them away and sat down on a cowskin and sulked.

'I'm hungry and thirsty and tired,' she said. 'Get me something to eat and drink.'

Her brother-in-law came home from hunting. Nyap stared at him rudely and didn't get up from her cowskin to greet him.

The days passed unhappily. Nyap never fetched the water or helped to pound the grain. She shouted at the children and quarrelled with her sister. She was rude to her brother-in-law and ate up all the nicest food. Weeks passed, and then months.

'Send her home,' the ogre said, 'before I do something terrible. I can't stand this woman in my hut any longer.'

Meanwhile, Nyakway was living happily at home with her parents. They had come to love her now that Nyap wasn't there.

'You're a good girl,' said her mother. 'I wish Nyap had a nice nature like yours.'

'It's a good thing we've got you,' her father said. 'What a pity that your sister isn't more like you.'

They were so pleased with Nyakway that they found her a rich husband. He was a good man, with many cows and a fine hut. Everything was agreed, and the wedding was planned.

It was on the very day of Nyakway's wedding that Nyap left her older sister's house and set off for home. Everyone was delighted to see her go. The children shouted and laughed and hoped she would never come back. Her sister smiled with relief, but she still made her a breakfast of delicious food to keep her satisfied all day long. Her brother-in-law the ogre didn't come to say goodbye. He was nowhere to be seen.

Nyap set off through the forest. She saw an eagle flying overhead, but she didn't know it was her brother-in-law. She caught sight of a bushbuck, bounding away through the trees, but she didn't realize it was the ogre.

Suddenly, she stopped. There, right ahead of her, was a beautiful tree. Ripe fruits hung from its branches, its leaves gleamed like gold and a delicious smell wafted from it.

'Nyap! Nyap!' the tree said. 'Come here and eat my fruit!'

'I certainly will,' said Nyap. 'I've been living in the house of an ugly, rude ogre, with dirty brown teeth and breath that stinks. They gave me hardly anything to eat and treated me badly from morning till night.'

She ran up to the tree, picked as many fruits as she could reach and crammed them into her mouth. Then she pushed roughly past the tree, breaking some of its delicate twigs, and went on, down the path. The tree changed back at once into the ogre. He ground his teeth (which were actually white and clean) with rage.

On and on walked Nyap. It was late now and the sun was going down. She began to hurry. Supper would be nearly ready at home, and all the best bits, she knew, would be for her.

Suddenly, she stopped. There, on the path ahead of her, was a delicious dish of fish, swimming in butter, with a magnificent spoon all ready beside it.

'Nyap! Nyap!' called out the dish. 'Aren't you hungry? Why don't you eat? I'm so delicious, you'll never taste anything so good again.'

Nyap didn't even bother to reply. She ran to the dish, sank down onto her knees, and began to gobble up the food as fast as she could.

'That's better,' she said as she finished the last bit and wiped her mouth. 'I'm half starved after staying with that dirty ogre and his naughty children. Why, I could hardly eat a thing while I was there. It quite put me off my food, seeing him stuff himself every day in such a disgusting way.'

She kicked the empty dish and spoon aside and walked on. At once, the ogre turned himself back into his own form. His eyes were red with rage and his teeth flashed white. He fell upon Nyap and tore her limb from limb, and ate her up.

Only her head rolled on down the path. It rolled and rolled, on and on, until it rolled right into her father's compound, and came to rest before his hut. The wedding guests jumped back in horror at the gruesome sight. Then the head opened its mouth and sang,

'I once was Nyap but now I'm dead,
And all that's left is my poor little head.
I'm rolling away as fast as I can
From that wicked, cruel, ogreish man.
Oh, sister Nyakway, you are the bride.
It should be me, with my man at my side.
Now you'll be happy, now you'll be rich,
While my head lies in a dusty ditch.
Catch me, bury me, give me peace,
Or I'll come and haunt you. I'll never cease.'

So Nyakway caught hold of Nyap's head, and it was buried, and that was the end of Nyap. But Nyakway and her husband lived happily ever after.

26

The Day the Sky Fell

Once there were two friends, a Sheep and a Goat, and they lived with their master, a cruel farmer. Every day, they saw the other farmers' flocks trotting away to a beautiful spring, which had the sweetest water and the longest green grass growing all around it.

But the Sheep and the Goat were never taken anywhere so fine. They had to find what grass they could on the bare, dusty roadside, and drink from nothing but a dirty puddle.

'I'm tired of living with our master,' said the Sheep.

'So am I,' answered the Goat. 'Let's run away.'

So the next night, when the farmer was sleeping, the Sheep and the Goat squeezed through a hole in the wall of the hut and ran away.

Dawn soon came, and they hurried on, afraid that the farmer would run after them and catch them.

They hadn't gone far when they met a lion.

'Aha!' said Lion. 'A Sheep and a Goat! Just what I fancy for my breakfast,' and he crouched down ready to spring.

'Stop!' said the Sheep. 'You must run away as fast as you can. The sky is about to fall on your head and the earth is going to split open under your feet!'

'Arrh!' roared the Lion in terror, and he ran away.

The Sheep and the Goat trotted on, but soon they met a leopard.

'Hmm,' said the Leopard. 'A Sheep and a Goat. Just when I was getting hungry,' and he licked his lips and got ready to pounce.

'Wait!' shouted the Goat. 'Run away! Don't stay here! The sky is about to fall on your head and the earth's going to split open under your feet!'

'Oh! Oh!' wailed the Leopard, and he ran away.

The Sheep and the Goat trotted on. After a while, they met a hyena.

'Oho,' laughed the Hyena. 'A Sheep and a Goat. Just what I feel like eating right now,' and he opened his mouth, ready to gobble them up.

'Don't!' yelled the Sheep. 'Save yourself! The sky is about to fall on your head and the earth's going to split open under your feet'.

'Wao! Wao!' howled the Hyena, and he ran away.

At last, the Sheep and the Goat came to the fine spring about which they had dreamed for so long. They ate the rich green grass and drank their fill of the sweet water. It was late in the afternoon now, and the sun was going down.

'It'll soon be dark,' said the Goat.

'I know,' answered the Sheep. 'I'm frightened. Where are we going to sleep tonight?'

'Don't worry,' the Goat said. 'There's a big tree over there. Let's climb up into its branches. Then we're sure to be safe.'

So the Sheep and the Goat climbed up into the branches of the tree.

They hadn't been there long, when, by chance, the Lion, the Leopard, and the Hyena arrived. The three big animals settled down under the tree to pass the night.

'I was badly tricked today,' the Lion said. 'I met a sheep and a goat and I was just about to kill them and eat them when they told me a silly story about the sky falling on my head. I must admit, it frightened me, and I ran away.'

'Well, there's a coincidence,' cried the Leopard. 'Exactly the same thing happened to me.'

'It happened to me too,' said the Hyena.

'If I ever get my hands on those two tricksters, I'll bite their heads off,' growled the Lion.

'I'll tear them to pieces,' roared the Leopard.

'I'll crunch up their bones,' howled the Hyena.

Up in the tree, the Sheep and the Goat trembled with terror.

'Be quiet,' whispered the Goat. 'Don't move or say a word. They won't know we're here.'

But the poor Sheep had drunk too much at the spring. She desperately needed to pee.

'I've got to pee,' she hissed to the Goat. 'I just can't wait.'

'Are you crazy?' answered the Goat. 'Didn't you hear what they want to do to us?'

'It's no good,' moaned the Sheep. 'I can't hang on any longer.'

'Cross your legs, then,' whispered the Goat. 'And wriggle and jiggle about. And don't, whatever you do, think of running water.'

So the Sheep tried not to think about running water, and she wriggled and jiggled about, and she began to cross her legs. But as she did so, her sharp little hoofs slipped off the branch and she fell down, right on top of the Lion, the Leopard, and the Hyena.

'The sky's falling! The sky's falling!' they all yelled, and they ran away in terror.

As for the Sheep and the Goat, they lived happily by the spring and ate the good grass and drank the sweet water ever after.

♫ *The Enchanted Flute* ♫

There was once a king who was just and wise and who was loved by all his people. He lived in a splendid house and wore beautiful clothes and was never seen without a magnificent turban on his head:

Whether the day was hot or cool, whether it rained or the wind blew, the turban stayed on the head of the King.

The people of the country were so used to seeing the King crowned with his turban that they never wondered about it at all. But the truth was that the turban hid a secret. On the King's head there was a birthmark, an ugly gash of pale skin, which he had had since the day he was born.

The King hid his birthmark night and day, and uncovered his head only when he bathed.

If people see the mark on my head, they'll think that I'm weak and sickly, he thought, and they won't respect me any more.

One day, as the King was taking his bath, a peddler happened to pass by. He heard the sound of splashing and, overcome by curiosity, peeped in through the window. Then he started back in amazement. He had seen the King without his turban and on his head was a large, pale birthmark.

So that's why the King always wears a turban, the man said to himself. He's afraid that people will see his birthmark!

He went on into the town and stopped for a drink at one of the local inns.

'Listen to this,' he said to the innkeeper. 'I've discovered the King's secret. Did you know that—'

'Stop! Don't say another word,' the innkeeper said. 'The King's secrets are his own and it's death to anyone who passes them on. Don't you know how tale-bearers are treated in these parts? They're carried up the mountain and taken to the edge of a cliff and the executioner swings his scimitar and slices off the tale-bearer's head, and his body falls over the cliff, and the hyenas and vultures rush to devour it.'

'What?' cried the poor peddler, trembling from head to foot. 'Is that really the penalty for telling a state secret?'

'Yes,' nodded the innkeeper. 'Why, only last week . . .'

But the peddler had heard enough and he ran out of the inn muttering to himself, 'I mustn't tell! I mustn't tell!'

Days passed, and the secret of the King's birthmark burned away inside the peddler. It burned in his head and it burned in his heart, it burned in his stomach and it burned in his intestines.

'I must tell someone,' he said, 'or I'll be burned alive.'

So he ran to the river, dug a hole at the water's edge, bent down and whispered into it, 'The King has a mark on his head! The king has a mark on his head!'

Then he filled the hole with earth and stood up. A smile spread

across his face. The burning secret had gone from inside him. He was free at last. Happily he went home.

Years passed, and where the peddler had dug a hole, a clump of tall reeds sprang up, with fine straight stalks and waving heads of green leaves.

One day, the King called his musicians.

'Tonight I'm giving a great feast,' he said, 'so prepare your best instruments and come and play for us.'

The musicians went to the river to cut fresh reeds to make pipes and flutes for the King's feast, and the longest and best reed of all was cut from the very clump that had grown from the hole in which the peddler had told the King's secret.

'What a fine flute this will make!' the musicians said happily, and

they took it back to the town.

Guests came to the King's feast from far and wide, and as they sat around him, enjoying the delicious food and strong honey mead, the King called his musicians.

'Start the music!' he cried.

The first singer took his place.

'Our King is like a lion,

He is brave and strong and true,' he sang.

The first flute-player lifted the flute to his lips and began to play the accompaniment, but instead of sweet flute music coming out of the reed, it began to sing in a loud voice all by itself:

'Our King has a mark on his head,

And he hides it night and day.'

The King's eyes went red with rage and he leapt from his chair.

'Take that man to the cliff!' he said. 'And cut off his head! Someone else must take his place.'

So the poor first flute-player was dragged away, and the second, trembling, raised the flute to his lips.

He had hardly begun to blow on it when the same loud voice sang out:

'The King has a mark on his head,

And he hides—'

'Stop him! Stop him!' roared the King, beside himself with anger. 'Take him away and cut off his head.'

The feast abruptly came to an end and all the guests crept away.

'Can it be true?' they whispered to each other. 'Does the King really have a birthmark on his head? Is that why he wears his turban both day and night and is never seen without it?'

Rumours flew around the country and the King, deeply worried, sent for his elders and advisers.

'Find out the truth,' he said. 'I want to know who is behind this mischief.'

Weeks passed. Then the elders and advisers returned to the King.

'Sire,' they said, 'the story is an old one and concerns a peddler who looked in at your window while you were bathing. He saw that on your head there was indeed a mark. Unable to keep the secret to himself, he dug a hole in the riverbank and whispered it into the ground. A clump of reeds grew up in that very spot and from it the flute-players cut one to make a flute. It was the flute that spoke, not the musicians. Look, here it is, sire. Try it for yourself.'

So the King put the flute to his lips and blew.

'The King has a mark on his . . .' it began to sing. The King stopped blowing at once. He was filled with remorse.

'I have executed innocent men,' he said. 'I should have known that the truth could never be hidden and that Mother Earth herself will speak it out at last. It is true. I have a mark on my head and I've had it all my life.'

Then he took off his turban and showed the birthmark to the people, and none of them laughed or thought the worse of him for it. From that time on, he was careful to be just in all things, and he regained the love of his people.

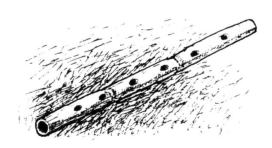

The Best Dream

*Once upon a time, three travellers were going on a
long journey. Two of them were big, tall men, but the
third was short and by no means as strong. The three
men had brought a goat with them on their journey,
which they intended to kill and eat for their dinner.*

Evening came, and the three men stopped to rest. They lit a fire, killed
the goat and put it in a pot to cook.

'It's a very small goat,' one of the big men whispered to the other. 'It
won't go far between the three of us.'

'That little fellow doesn't need as much food as we do,' said the other
big man. 'Let's trick him.'

So as the meat was cooking, the first big man said, 'I've got a good
idea. There's only enough meat to make a good meal for one of us, so
let's all go to sleep now. In the night we're sure to dream. We'll tell each

38

other our dreams in the morning and whoever has the most beautiful dream will have all the meat for himself.'

The others agreed and they all lay down to sleep, but the little man saw the others winking and smiling at each other.

They're trying to fool me, he thought.

'Goodnight, my friends,' he said. 'I'll ask God to send me a good dream. Sleep well,' and he lay down under the stars and shut his eyes.

After a while he heard snores coming from the two big men. He went to the first one and said in his ear, 'There's a scorpion under your foot.'

The first big man didn't move. The little man went to the second big man.

'There is a snake coiled round your arm,' he said.

The second big man didn't stir. The little man smiled.

They really are asleep, he said to himself.

Very quietly, he crept over to the pot sitting by the fire, took out the meat and ate it, licking his lips, for it was very good. Then he put the bones back into the pot, went back to his place and fell fast asleep.

In the morning they all woke up.

'Oh,' said the first big man, stretching himself, 'I had such a beautiful dream. God himself took me to paradise, and he showed me its marvels and beauties and we talked together.'

'And I,' said the second big man, 'had a wonderful dream too. I went to Mecca and met the prophet Mohammed, and I sat with him and we talked to each other.'

'You were lucky,' the little man said. 'I had a terrible dream. A big strong fellow came up to me and put his foot on my neck. Then he reached over to the pot, took the meat out and ate it. All that was left was the bones.'

The two big men rushed over to the pot and looked inside it.

'It wasn't a dream!' the first man cried. 'The meat has gone! Someone has been here and eaten it all! Why didn't you wake me?'

'Oh, I tried, I tried,' the little man said, 'but you were in paradise with God. You didn't hear me.'

'You could have woken me,' the second man said.

'But I shouted and yelled at you,' said the little man. 'You were in Mecca, with the prophet Mohammed. You couldn't hear a thing.'

The Bull Who Gave Birth to a Calf

The Lion and the Ostrich were great friends. They were farmers and they lived together in the same house and shared all the work between them.

The Lion's most precious possession was a bull. Every day, he took it out to the pasture lands to graze, and he looked after it carefully all day long.

The Ostrich had a prize cow. Every day she took her cow out into the countryside and guarded it against danger.

One day, the Lion looked at the Ostrich's cow and saw that it was pregnant. All that day, he was quiet and thoughtful, and when the evening came he said to the Ostrich, 'You look tired, my dear Ostrich. Why don't you stay at home and rest tomorrow? I'll take your cow out with my bull and look after them both together.'

'That's very kind of you,' said the Ostrich. 'I am feeling a little tired today. A rest would do me good.'

So the next day the Lion took the cow and the bull out together, and the Ostrich stayed at home.

That very day, out in the countryside, the cow gave birth to a fine calf. The Lion looked after them well and when the evening came he set off for home. On the way he found a grindstone lying by the path. He picked it up and took it with him.

'Ostrich!' he shouted as his hut came into sight. 'I've got some wonderful news. My bull has given birth to a calf! And that's not all. Your cow has given birth to a fine new grindstone. Come and see!'

The Ostrich came out of the hut and looked at him in amazement.

'What do you mean, your bull has given birth to a calf?' she said. 'Such a thing is completely impossible. It was my cow that produced the calf, and so the calf is mine. And where did you get this old grindstone from? I don't want it. I want my calf.'

'The calf's not yours. It's mine,' said the Lion.

'No, it's mine,' said the Ostrich.

'How dare you speak to me like that?' said the Lion.

'How dare you try to cheat me?' cried the Ostrich.

They quarrelled loudly for a long time.

'I'll call a meeting of all the animals,' the Ostrich said at last. 'They can decide between us.'

So she called all the animals together. Only the Fox refused to come.

'Pass judgement between you and the Lion?' he said. 'Not me. But I tell you what, I'll run past the meeting and call out my opinion as I go.'

'Listen to this, neighbours,' said the Ostrich, when all the animals had gathered together for the meeting. 'I'll tell you what's happened and you can decide which of us is right. The Lion took our animals out to graze today, and my cow gave birth to a calf. But the Lion said it was the bull that gave birth, and he claims that the calf is his.'

The other animals all looked at the Lion, waiting for him to speak,

but he merely opened his big red mouth in a majestic yawn and they saw his strong white teeth.

'I think . . . I think the calf belongs to the Lion,' squeaked a nervous mouse.

'So do we, so do we,' chorused all the other animals.

'You see?' said the Lion, shaking his mane. 'I was in the right all along.'

'Wait a minute,' the Ostrich said. 'There's one animal who isn't here. We can't agree until everyone's had their say. Fox! Fox! Where are you?'

The Fox appeared on the high road above the meeting place.

'I'm sorry,' he said. 'I can't stop now. I've just had news that my father's giving birth to some cubs. I must run and help him.'

All the animals burst out laughing.

'Don't be ridiculous!' growled the Lion. 'Your father can't give birth to cubs. That's nonsense.'

'How can you say such a thing?' said the Fox. 'If your bull can give birth to a calf, why can't my father give birth to cubs?'

The animals laughed louder than ever, and the Lion was so angry that he jumped up and began to chase the Fox, who ran safely away to his den.

The Lion didn't dare to show his face again, in case the animals laughed at him, and he went away. But the Ostrich kept her calf and lived happily ever after.

The King of the Forest

Once there were four brave hunters from the tribe of Afar, and they lived in a village near a very big forest.

Now the forest was full of wild hyenas, and it was ruled by their King who was strong and cunning and who terrified everyone who went near him.

One day the brothers said to each other, 'We're not afraid of the hyenas. Let's go into the forest and explore it.'

So into the forest they went.

They hadn't gone far when a gang of fierce hyenas surrounded them. Without a word they took the four brothers to face their King, the biggest hyena any of them had ever seen.

45

The Hyena King looked at the men and said, 'How dare you come into my forest? You know that we hyenas will kill and eat anyone who comes near us. Who do you think is going to save you from us?' Then he turned to the oldest brother and said, 'You! Speak first!'

The first brother spoke up boldly.

'God, the Creator of the world, will save me,' he said. 'He knows the day of my birth, and the day of my death has already been written in his great book. I trust in him.'

The Hyena King turned to the second brother.

'Now you!' he said.

The second brother stepped forward.

'I am Afari,' he said proudly, 'and I'm not afraid of anyone. My clansmen are bold and fierce, and if you kill me they won't let me die in vain. If you touch a hair of my head they will come into your forest and they won't rest until they've had their revenge. I trust in the men of my tribe.'

'Now you,' said the King of the Hyenas, turning to the third brother. 'What have you to say?'

'I put my trust in Mother Earth,' said the third brother. 'She gave birth to me, and I eat the food and drink the water that she provides. When I die, I shall be buried in her. I'm relying on Mother Earth.'

The fourth brother didn't wait for the Hyena King to speak to him. He ran forward and said, 'Oh great King! Everyone knows how wonderful you are, how good and generous and just. Your fame has spread far and wide throughout the whole country. I do not believe that you would eat a poor worm like me. And even if you are tempted, I have friends among the hyenas, O King. They'll stand by me if I'm in trouble. I'm relying on your great goodness, and on my hyena friends.'

Then he stepped back to stand with his brothers.

The King of the Hyenas called out to his soldiers, 'Look at this one, the oldest brother. He relies on God, his Creator. But God also knows the day of our births, and our deaths, too, are written in his book. We have no quarrel with God, so we must let him go.'

Then he pointed to the second brother and said, 'This brave Afari knows the men of his clan. It's true that if we attack him his kinsmen will hunt us down. We have no quarrel with his clan, so he can go.'

He turned to the third brother.

'This man puts his trust in Mother Earth,' he said. 'But we too live on the earth. We eat the food and drink the water that she provides. How can we quarrel with her? He too can go.'

Then he looked at the fourth brother.

'You fool,' he said. 'You think you can flatter me into letting you go, and you rely on your friends among us. But you have forgotten that we are hyenas. Your friends here may try to save you, but we'll happily attack each other for the honour of eating you. It's our nature to fight among ourselves, and it's our nature to eat people too.'

And with that the hyenas began to fight over the fourth brother, and they fell on him and ate him, but the others went home safely to their village.

Abba Bollo and the Necklace

*Once upon a time there was a little girl who had
a pretty necklace. One day, she went down to the
river to fetch some water and there she met a
boy called Bollo.*

'You've got a pretty necklace,' said Bollo. 'Let me look at it.'

So the little girl took off her necklace and gave it to Bollo, who looked at it and looked at it.

'Who wants a silly necklace?' he said, and he threw it into the water.

The little girl was very angry.

'Why did you do that?' she cried. 'Dive in and get it back for me.'

'No,' said Bollo. 'I won't.' And he ran away.

The little girl ran to find Abba Bollo, Bollo's father.

'Abba Bollo,' she said. 'Please beat your son for me.'

'Why should I do that?' said Abba Bollo.

'Because he took my necklace, and looked at it and looked at it, and threw it into the river,' said the little girl.

'I won't beat him for that,' said Abba Bollo.

The little girl ran home again, and on the way she passed a tree stump.

'Tree stump,' she said. 'When Abba Bollo comes this way, please trip him up for me.'

'Why should I do that?' said the tree stump.

'Because he won't beat Bollo, and Bollo won't give me back my necklace, which he looked at and looked at and threw into the river,' said the little girl.

'I won't trip him up for that,' said the tree stump.

On went the little girl, and soon she met a mole.

'Mole,' she said. 'Please burrow into the ground and eat the roots of the tree stump.'

'Why should I do that?' said the mole.

'Because the tree stump won't trip up Abba Bollo, and Abba Bollo

won't beat Bollo, and Bollo won't give me back my necklace, which he looked at and looked at and threw into the river,' said the little girl.

'I wouldn't eat the tree stump for that,' said the mole.

The little girl was angry now, and she went to the fire that glowed in the hearth. She said to it, 'Fire, please burn the mole.'

'Why should I do that?' said the fire.

'Because the mole won't eat the roots of the stump, and the stump won't trip up Abba Bollo, and Abba Bollo won't beat Bollo, and Bollo won't give me back my necklace, which he looked at and looked at and threw into the river,' said the little girl.

'I wouldn't burn the mole for that,' said the fire.

The little girl stamped her foot and ran to the water pot and said, 'Water, please put out the fire.'

'Why should I do that?' said the water.

'Because the fire won't burn the mole, and the mole won't eat the roots of the stump, and the stump won't trip up Abba Bollo, and Abba Bollo won't beat Bollo, and Bollo won't give me back my necklace,

which he looked at and looked at and threw into the river,' said the little girl.

'I wouldn't put the fire out for that,' said the water.

So the little girl rushed into the forest and there she found an elephant.

'Elephant,' she said, 'please drink the water.'

'Why should I do that?' said the elephant.

'Because the water won't put out the fire, and the fire won't burn the mole, and the mole won't eat the roots of the stump, and the stump won't trip up Abba Bollo, and Abba Bollo won't beat Bollo, and Bollo won't give me back my necklace, which he looked at and looked at and threw into the river,' said the little girl.

'I wouldn't drink the water for that,' said the elephant.

The little girl shouted at the elephant but he would not do as she asked, so she ran to the herdsmen who were tending their cattle.

'Herdsmen,' she said, 'please hunt the elephant.'

'Why should we do that?' said the herdsmen.

'Because the elephant won't drink the water, and the water won't put out the fire, and the fire won't burn the mole, and the mole won't eat the roots of the stump, and the stump won't trip up Abba Bollo, and Abba Bollo won't beat Bollo, and Bollo won't give me back my necklace, which he looked at and looked at and threw into the river,' said the little girl.

'We wouldn't hunt the elephant for that,' said the herdsmen.

'You'll be sorry!' said the little girl and she ran up to a giant tree.

'Tree,' said the little girl, 'please fall on the herdsmen.'

'Why should I do that?' said the tree.

'Because the herdsmen won't hunt the elephant, and the elephant won't drink the water, and the water won't put out the fire, and the fire won't burn the mole, and the mole won't eat the roots of the stump, and the stump won't trip up Abba Bollo, and Abba Bollo won't beat Bollo, and Bollo won't give me back my necklace, which he looked at and looked at and threw into the river,' said the little girl.

'I wouldn't fall on the herdsmen for that,' said the tree.

The little girl was so cross that she stamped her foot and danced with rage and shouted and yelled all at the same time. Then she went to the axe and said, 'Axe, please cut down the tree.'

'Why should I do that?' said the axe.

'Because the tree won't fall on the herdsmen, and the herdsmen won't hunt the elephant, and the elephant won't drink the water, and the water won't put out the fire, and the fire won't burn the mole, and the mole won't eat the roots of the stump, and the stump won't trip up Abba Bollo, and Abba Bollo won't beat Bollo, and Bollo won't give me back my necklace, which he looked at and looked at and threw into the river,' said the little girl.

'This is terrible!' said the axe. 'Don't worry, little girl. I'll help you.'

So the axe jumped up and hit the tree, and the tree began to fall on the herdsmen, and the herdsmen picked up their spears to hunt the elephant, and the elephant lowered his trunk into the water, and the water spilled over to put out the fire, and the fire shot out its flames towards the mole, and the mole started gnawing the roots of the tree stump, and the stump tripped up Abba Bollo, and Abba Bollo began to beat his son.

And Bollo ran to the river, and dived in, and pulled out the necklace and gave it back to the little girl.

'Thank you,' she said.

 The Jackal and the Rabbit

*A Jackal was burrowing into a hillside, looking for
something good to eat, when a big boulder rolled
down on to his paw, pinning him to the ground. The
Jackal pushed and pulled and clawed and scrabbled
but try as he might he couldn't release his paw.*

He began shouting at the top of his voice.

'Help! Help! Someone please come and help me!'

A Rabbit heard his cries and came up to see what the matter was.

'Oh Rabbit,' said the Jackal. 'Please help me. Roll this boulder off my
paw. If you do, you'll save my life and I'll be grateful to you for ever
and ever.'

'Hmm,' said the Rabbit. 'I'll try, but I'm only a little animal, and
rather weak. It will take me a long time to shift this boulder. What will
you give me in return for all my trouble?'

'Food!' said the Jackal. 'I'll give you food. I'll prepare a wonderful feast for you, and let you eat until you're bursting.'

So the Rabbit pushed and pulled and clawed and scrabbled at the boulder until at last he managed to move it and release the Jackal's paw.

But as soon as the Jackal was free, he sprang up, and caught the Rabbit in his jaws and said, 'Now I'm going to eat you.'

'No, no!' cried the Rabbit. 'You ungrateful creature. I've just saved you from a long, lingering death, and you promised to reward me. How can you treat me like this?'

'I must,' said the Jackal. 'I'm faint with hunger. If I don't eat you I'll die anyway.'

At that moment, an old man passed by. The Rabbit called out to him.

'Please, old man,' he said, 'come and judge our case. The Jackal was trapped under a boulder, and he promised me a feast if I would only free him. So I pushed and pulled and clawed and scrabbled until I'd set him free. But he jumped on me straight away and now he says he's going to eat me.'

'That's not right at all,' the old man said. 'The Rabbit did you a good turn, Jackal. You must set him free.'

The Jackal was furious and he bared his sharp teeth and growled at the old man.

'How dare you talk to me like that?' he snarled. 'I'll eat the Rabbit first, and then I'll eat you too.'

The old man opened his eyes wide, so that he looked frightened.

'Oho,' he said. 'It's like that, is it? How very fierce you are, to be sure. Well, perhaps I spoke too hastily. Maybe you were right after all. It's difficult for me to decide without seeing what actually happened. You were trapped under a boulder, you say? Where was it exactly?'

'Here! It was here!' said the Jackal eagerly, running back to the boulder.

The old man walked round the boulder and looked at it closely, shaking his head doubtfully.

'Let me see,' he said. 'Where were you precisely when the boulder ran on to your paw?'

'Here! Here!' said the Jackal impatiently, standing right under the boulder again.

The old man looked at the boulder, then he looked at the Rabbit. He scratched his chin and shook his head doubtfully.

'It's a very big boulder,' he said, 'and you're only a weak little animal. How did you manage to roll it off the Jackal's paw?'

'Like this! Like this!' said the Rabbit proudly, and he pushed the boulder with all his might until it rolled back on to the Jackal's paw and trapped him again.

'Ah,' said the old man. 'I see it all now. This was how you found the Jackal?'

'Yes,' panted the Rabbit.

'Just like this,' nodded the Jackal.

'That's just fine, then,' said the old man. 'I can see exactly how it happened. And now, Rabbit, you and I can go on our way again, and leave this ungrateful animal right where he is.'

The Baboon's Headband

A troup of baboons once had a strong leader. He was vain and selfish. He made all the other baboons praise and admire him all day long, and if they didn't, he beat them cruelly.

One day, some of the smaller baboons went to the chief and said, 'O great and everlasting chief, we know, of course, that you are the finest and biggest and noblest of us all, but sometimes, when we're all together in the forest, we can't immediately tell if it's you or another baboon who's giving us orders. We humbly beseech your lordship to wear something special so that we can see at a glance that it's your majesty who's commanding us and not some other dumb animal.'

The chief of the baboons considered the idea.

'What sort of thing do you suggest?' he said.

'What about a headband?' the other baboons said. 'We've found a nice piece of rope on the forest floor. Let your worthless subjects tie it round your grace's head.'

'All right,' said the chief, 'but if I graciously consent to wear this headband as you suggest, I shall expect absolute obedience, do you hear? Whatever I tell you to do, you must do. Wherever I go, you must follow me. Do you understand, you stupid, worthless animals?'

'Oh yes! Oh yes, great king!' said all the other baboons, falling over themselves as they bowed and scraped to the chief.

'Very well,' said the chief.

So the baboons tied the rope round their chief's head, and sat back to admire the effect. The chief pretended to be unconcerned, and he stood up on his hind legs and yawned.

All the other baboons stood up and yawned too.

The chief started swinging from branch to branch through the trees. The other baboons meekly followed him.

The chief stopped, sat down, and scratched himself. All the other baboons silently did the same.

After a while, the headband on the chief's head began to feel uncomfortable. He put his hands up and tried to undo the knot. All the other baboons pretended to do the same.

But the knot was too tight for the chief. He couldn't undo it. He sat down on a high rock and put his head in his hands.

'This headband's too tight,' he said. 'I've got a headache.'

All the other baboons sat down and put their heads in their hands.

'This headband's too tight,' they said. 'I've got a headache.'

The chief was angry. He stood up and glared at the other baboons.

'I'm serious!' he cried. 'Get this thing off me!'

The other baboons all stood up and glared too.

'I'm serious!' they cried. 'Get this thing off me!'

The chief clutched his head. He was so angry, his head was swelling and the headband felt tighter and tighter.

'It's killing me!' he shouted.

'It's killing me!' shouted all the other baboons.

Then the chief toppled backwards off the big rock, and the other baboons fell on top of him and crushed him with their weight so that he died.

And that was the end of a vain tyrant.

The Rat King's Son

There was once a colony of rats who
were proud and arrogant.

'There's no one to beat us,' they said to each other. 'We're the greatest, most magnificent and exceptional animals in the whole wide world.'

The rats had a king who was the most high and mighty of them all, and the king's eldest son was just as bad as his father.

'Never forget, my son,' the Rat King would say. 'There's no one on earth or in heaven who is as good as me. Or you.'

The time came for the Rat King to find a bride for his son.

'What are we going to do?' he said to his counsellors. 'There's no animal on this miserable earth who is good enough to marry my son.'

'You're right, sire,' his counsellors cried eagerly. 'No one on earth is good enough for our glorious prince.'

'Then we must look above,' cried the Rat King. 'Go to our Creator and ask him for his daughter's hand in marriage.'

So the counsellors went to the Creator and when they had come into his presence they said to him, 'My Lord, you must have heard tell of the handsome, intelligent, and most noble prince of rats. We have come to ask you to give us your daughter to be his bride.'

The Creator smiled, and said, 'I can tell from what you say that your prince is a most extraordinary young rat. In fact, I'm sure he's so wonderful that not even my daughter would be good enough for him.'

'Who could be better than the daughter of the Creator?' said the Rat King's counsellors, looking puzzled.

'There's one who is greater than me,' said the Creator. 'I live in the sky. Fog comes and wraps itself around me, choking me so that I can hardly breathe. I can't make it come or make it go. Ask the Fog to give his daughter to your prince.'

The counsellors returned to their king and told him what the Creator had said.

'Well,' the Rat King said. 'What the Creator says must be so. Go and ask the fog to give his daughter to my son.'

Off went the counsellors to find the Fog. They came to his misty palace and said to him, 'Sir, our great prince wants to marry your beautiful daughter.'

'Tell me more about him,' said the Fog.

'Words cannot describe him,' the counsellors began.

'In that case,' said the Fog, 'he's much too fine a fellow for my daughter and he should marry someone greater than her.'

The counsellors looked bewildered.

'Who can be greater than the Fog?' they said. 'Even our Creator claims you are more powerful than him. You wrap yourself around him until he can hardly breathe.'

'Oh, the Wind is greater than I am,' said the Fog. 'It blows me away

and scatters me to pieces until not one scrap of me remains. Go to the Wind and ask him to give his daughter to your prince.'

The counsellors returned to their king and told him what the Fog had said.

'Well,' the Rat King said. 'What the Fog says must be so. Go and ask the Wind to give his daughter to my son.'

Off went the counsellors to find the Wind. They came upon him roaring on the mountain tops, and they shouted out to him, 'Sir, we have come from the Rat King who wants your daughter to marry his son.'

'Tell me more about him,' said the Wind.

'Our prince is beyond description,' the counsellors began.

'Oh my,' said the Wind. 'He sounds much too good for my daughter. You must ask someone greater than me.'

'Who can be greater than the Wind?' the counsellors said. 'Even the Fog knows you are stronger than him. You blow him away and scatter him to pieces until not one scrap of him remains.'

'Oh,' said the Wind, 'the Mountain is greater than I am. I hit him and buffet him with all my might but he doesn't move an inch. Go and ask the Mountain to give his daughter to your prince.'

The counsellors returned to their king and told him what the Wind had said.

'Well,' the Rat King said. 'What the Wind says must be so. Go and ask the Mountain to give his daughter to my son.'

Off went the counsellors to speak to the Mountain. They climbed his steep slopes and arrived at last on his high and lonely summit.

'Mountain,' they said, 'we have come from the Rat King, who wants your daughter to marry his son.'

'Describe him to me,' said the Mountain.

'How can we possibly describe someone so wonderful?' the counsellors cried.

'Ah,' said the Mountain. 'Your prince is clearly much too noble a person to marry my poor daughter. You must find someone greater than me.'

'Who can be greater than the Mountain?' said the counsellors. 'Even the wind knows you are stronger than him. He hits you and buffets you with all his might but you don't move an inch.'

'Go to the Bushrats,' said the Mountain. 'They dig and burrow into my side and carve out nests for themselves under my foundations. The Bushrats are greater than I am.'

The counsellors returned to their king and told him what the Mountain had said. The Rat King puffed out his chest and strutted about proudly.

'The Bushrats are our cousins,' he said happily. 'If they are the greatest of all, then we are too, and it's only right and proper that my son should marry their daughter.'

So the Rat King's son married the Bushrat's daughter and they lived together happily, contented with their lot, convinced to the end of their days that they were the greatest creatures in all the world.

The Shield of Kindness

*Once upon a time, there was a good old man who
had three sons. They were fine and brave and he
loved them dearly.*

The family's happiness was spoiled only by the deceit and greed of
their neighbour, a wicked merchant, who constantly tried to steal from
them, and even threatened their lives.

One day the old man realized that he was about to die. He called his
sons to him and said to them, 'My dear children, I have lived a long and
happy life, but my death is now approaching. Before I die, I want to
give you my blessing and pass over to you everything I possess, my
cattle, my fields, my trees, and my huts. Share them equally among
yourselves.'

The sons were sad when they heard this, and they turned to go out
of the hut, but their father called them back.

'Look,' he said, 'hanging up there on the wall above my head is my father's shield. It belonged to his father and his grandfather before him and it's the most precious thing I own. Only one of you can inherit it.'

The three sons looked at him hopefully. All of them wanted to inherit their father's shield.

'I'm going to give you a test,' the old man said. 'You are all three good and strong and brave, but the greatest quality of all is kindness. I want you to go out and perform a kind deed. Come and tell me what you've done, and whoever has shown himself to be the kindest of all will inherit the family shield.'

The three sons went away and travelled far and wide through the whole land of Ethiopia, looking for the chance to do a kind deed. At last they returned to their father's hut.

'Well, my sons?' he said. 'Tell me what you've done.'

'Father,' the oldest one said, 'in my travels, I went all the way to the sources of the Nile, and as I stood at the very place where the great river leaves Lake Tana, I saw a woman standing by the bank, shouting

and crying because her baby had fallen into the water. The river was deep there, and infested with crocodiles, but I risked my life and jumped in and rescued the baby. Wasn't that an act of kindness?'

'It was indeed,' said his father. 'You did well. But you were acting only as any human being should do. No one could have stood back and let a baby die. Now, my second son, what have you done?'

'Well, father,' the second son said, 'I too travelled far from home. One day, as I passed through a deep valley, where leopards lurked among the rocks and vultures circled overhead, I met a man who was carrying a hundred silver dollars. He wanted to go to the market to buy food, so he said to me, "My friend, please take care of my money for me, and don't let anyone steal it while I'm gone." So I waited while he went to the market and when he came back I returned all his money to him. "You're an honest man," he said. "Take ten silver dollars as a reward." But I refused. "The money's yours," I said. "Keep it." Now, father, wasn't that kind of me?'

'You are indeed honest, and brave too,' the old man said, 'and you showed that you have no great love of money, but that isn't real kindness. Now, my third son, tell us what you have done.'

His third son said, 'I walked for many miles, across deserts and plains, until I came to the high mountains. I rested in a desolate place, at the top of a great cliff, where hyenas howled and eagles swooped down on their prey. Suddenly I saw our old neighbour, the merchant, who tried so often to steal all our property and even threatened our lives. He was lying close to the edge of the abyss, fast asleep, in danger of rolling over to his death. If I'd called out to him suddenly and

70

woken him up he would have been terrified, thinking I wanted to attack him, and he would have jumped back and fallen over the cliff. So I took hold of him gently, and before he was fully awake, I dragged him away from danger and left him in a field to sleep in safety.'

His father was very pleased when he heard this.

'My son, you did very well,' he said. 'Your act was one of true kindness. This man has been a curse to us and our family for many years, and yet you didn't take revenge on him but saved his life.'

So the old man gave the shield to his third son, because he had learned the true meaning of kindness.

The Shepherd Boy At School

Once there was a shepherd boy who started going to school. He found his lessons very difficult, and the hardest one of all was Maths.

'Take 3 from 5,' the teacher said. 'What's the answer?'
  The boy shook his head.

  'What's 4 minus 2?' asked the teacher. 'You must be able to do that one.'

  But the boy couldn't.

  'Well,' the teacher said. 'Here's an example you ought to understand. Say you have five sheep in your fold and one of them runs out through a

72

hole in the fence. How many will you have left?'

'That's easy,' the shepherd boy answered. 'I won't have any left.'

'How can you be so stupid?' answered the teacher.

'I'm not stupid!' said the boy. 'I don't know much about Maths, but I know all about sheep. If one goes out through a hole in the fence, all the others will follow!'

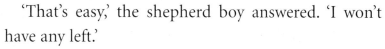

The Man Who Grew Feathers

Once there was a rich old man who had two sons. The eldest, who was his father's favourite, was proud and selfish. The younger son was good-hearted and full of kindness, but his father didn't care for him at all.

The time came for the old man to die, and he was buried with his fathers. He left instructions that all his wealth, his land, his huts, and his three cowsheds full of cattle should go to his elder son. Nothing was left for the younger son but a rooster, a big bird with fine red feathers.

Harvest time came, and the elder brother gathered in his crops and filled his grain stores until they were overflowing, but he never gave any grain to the younger man.

'It can't be helped,' the younger brother said to his wife. 'No doubt he needs all the grain for himself.'

The rich brother sometimes killed a cow and gave feasts for his friends, but he never invited his brother.

'Ah well,' the younger brother said. 'He is still my brother, after all.'

Then, one day, the elder brother fell ill. He sent for the medicine man who came to examine him.

'You won't get better,' the medicine man said, 'unless you eat the flesh of a big rooster with fine red feathers.'

'I haven't got a rooster,' the sick man cried.

'No, but your brother has,' said his wife. 'That horrid thing! It wakes me up every morning with its ugly crowing.'

'Then go and ask my brother to give it to me,' the older brother moaned. 'And hurry up. I feel so ill I'm sure I'm about to die.'

His wife ran to the younger brother's house.

'Your elder brother's ill,' she said, 'and the only thing that can cure him is the flesh of a big rooster with fine red feathers.'

'Husband,' said the younger brother's wife. 'That rooster is the only thing we have.'

Her husband frowned at her.

'If my brother needs it, he must have it,' he said.

So he gave the rooster to his brother's wife, and she took it away and killed it and gave its meat to the sick man to eat.

Very soon the elder brother began to feel better.

'Slaughter a cow,' he said to his wife. 'Make a feast. Invite my friends. Let's celebrate my recovery.'

But he didn't invite his brother.

The feast was at its height and everyone was sitting at their ease, enjoying the tasty stews, when the elder brother felt that something strange was happening to him. He touched his legs and felt his arms.

'Help!' he shouted. 'What's happening to me? I'm growing feathers!'

His wife and all his guests jumped up in horror. It was true. Fine red feathers were growing all over the body of their host.

75

The medicine man and the elders came running as soon as they heard the news. They sat down together to discuss the problem.

'You've been greedy,' they said at last to the sick man. 'You took everything that your father left you and gave nothing to your brother. You even took his rooster, his only possession, without a word of thanks, although he gave it to you freely and generously. You will be cursed and your feathers will grow until he has forgiven you.'

At once the elder brother went to the younger brother and begged his forgiveness.

'Brother, forgive me,' he said. 'I've been selfish and greedy, and I took all you had without a word of thanks.'

His younger brother embraced him affectionately.

'Of course I forgive you,' he said, 'for we are brothers, after all.'

At once the feathers dropped off the elder brother and he had a man's skin again. He shared his property equally with his younger brother, and from that time on they lived in harmony with each other.

The Monkey's Birthday

The Hyena, the Fox, and the Monkey all lived together. They fetched wood for each other and cooked each other's food and went out hunting every day.

One day, they found four cows wandering about in the forest so they took them home.

'We're rich now,' said the Hyena. 'We've got four cows.'

'Yes,' the Fox answered. 'There's one for the Hyena, one for the Monkey, and one for me.'

'And one left over,' the Monkey said. 'Who's going to have that one?'

They talked about it for a long time, and at last they agreed that the cow should belong to whichever of them was the oldest.

'Oh, I'm sure I'm the oldest,' the Hyena said. 'I was born years and years ago. Years before that, even. Endless years ago. In the years before there were years.' 'Hmm,' said the Monkey. 'You're not as old as me, then, because I was born on the very day when the earth and the sky were made.'

'You're quite right,' laughed the Fox. 'So you were. Your parents gave a wonderful party to celebrate your birth. Your grandmother, who was an old friend of mine, made the best wheat cakes I've ever tasted. Oh, I remember it so well!'

'Really?' said the Hyena and the Monkey. 'Then you're the oldest of us, Fox.'

'Why, so I am,' smiled the Fox, and he took the fourth cow for himself.

The Fox and the Crow

A fox was busy outside her house one day, spreading out her grain to dry in the sun. She ran down to the stream to fetch some water and while she was gone a crow came and pecked at her grain.

'Thief! Go away!' shouted the Fox, running up as fast as she could. 'Leave my grain alone!'

But the Crow flapped his wings and flew away.

The Fox guarded the grain for a while, then she went into her house to tend the fire. When she had gone, the Crow came again and ate some more grain.

'Rascal! How dare you?' shouted the Fox, rushing at the Crow and trying to catch him in her jaws. 'Leave my grain alone!'

But the Crow was too quick for her. He flapped his wings and flew away.

So it went on all day long. While the Fox guarded her grain the Crow stayed away, but as soon as the Fox's back was turned, down he swooped and pecked and gobbled as fast as he could.

The Fox grew angrier and angrier.

'I'll get that Crow,' she said to herself.

The next morning, she got up early and hid herself behind the house. As soon as the Crow came down to steal the grain, she jumped out and caught him in her paws.

'Oh! Oh!' said the Crow. 'Let me go! Please let me go!'

'Why should I?' said the Fox. 'You're a thief. You've been stealing my grain, and now I'm going to punish you.'

'Oh yes,' said the Crow. 'You're right. I'm a thief and I'm wicked and I deserve to be punished as much as you like. Do whatever you want to me but I beg you, if you have any mercy in your heart, don't, don't throw me into the bushes!'

'Throw you into the bushes?' said the Fox. 'Why should I do that? No, no, I'm going to make a fire and boil some water, and cook you in my pot.'

'Yes! Oh yes!' cried the Crow. 'Make a fire and boil some water and cook me if you like, but don't, don't throw me into the bushes!'

The Fox looked thoughtful.

'Maybe I won't make a fire after all,' she said. 'Maybe I'll just fetch my axe and chop off your head.'

'That will be fine by me,' croaked the Crow. 'Fetch your axe and chop off my head as much as you like, but please, oh please, don't throw me into the bushes!'

The Fox thought even harder. Then she laughed.

'Well, my friend,' she said. 'You've shown me yourself what I should do. Since you're so afraid of the bushes, that's just where I'm going to throw you,' and she flung the Crow right into the bushes.

At once the Crow flew out of the bushes and away to safety.

'You fool, Fox!' he called out. 'You should never believe a thief!'

The Clever Wife

*Once there was an ignorant man who had a very
clever wife. She knew the answer to every question
and he relied on her for everything. The woman
loved her husband dearly and they lived
happily together for many years.*

Not far away from the couple lived a clever man. He was rich and
powerful. Everyone was afraid of him and did his bidding.

The clever man watched his neighbour's wife and saw that she was
not only beautiful but good and clever too.

I want her for myself, he thought.

He went to his neighbour's house and said, 'Your wife's a clever
woman, but you're just a stupid fellow. I, on the other hand, am a very
clever man. Your wife should be married to me. Divorce her, and give
her to me.'

The ignorant man looked worried.

'You are indeed a very clever fellow,' he said, 'and I know that my wife's much cleverer than me, but I love her all the same. I'd really rather stay with her.'

'We must take the matter to the judge,' said the clever man. 'Let him decide between us.'

So, with a heavy heart, the ignorant man went with his clever neighbour to the judge, and they explained the matter to him.

'Why do you say this man is ignorant?' the judge asked the clever man.

'Ask him any question you like,' the clever man said contemptuously. 'He won't be able to answer any of them.'

'Very well, sir,' said the judge, who was afraid of the clever man himself. He turned to the ignorant man and said, 'I'll ask you two questions. The first is this: how many stars are there in the sky? And the second is this: where is the navel of the earth?'

The ignorant man sighed. I've lost my wife, he thought. These questions are too hard for me.

'Take your time,' the judge said. 'Come back tomorrow and give me your answers then.'

The ignorant man hurried home, his brow creased with anxiety. He waited until night had fallen, then he went outside and tried to count the stars. Hour after hour he stared at the sky but try as he might he couldn't count them all.

At last his wife came out to look for him.

'Husband, what are you doing?' she said. 'What's the matter?'

'The judge has asked me some questions,' the man said, 'and if I can't answer them I shall lose you to my neighbour.'

'Tell me what the questions are,' his wife said.

'How many stars are there in the sky? And where is the navel of the earth?' the poor man said.

'I'll tell you how to answer,' said his wife. 'Come in now and eat your supper. It's waiting for you.'

The next day, she gave her husband a sack of wheat and a stick, and the ignorant man and the clever man returned to the judge.

'Well?' the judge said. 'Have you found the answers to my questions? How many stars are there in the sky?'

The ignorant man tipped out his sack of wheat on to the ground.

'There are as many stars in the sky as there are grains of wheat in this sack,' he said, 'and if you don't believe me try and count them yourself.'

'And where,' asked the judge, 'is the navel of the earth?'

The ignorant man plunged his stick into the ground.

'The navel of the earth is here,' he said. 'And if you don't believe me, dig until you find it.'

The judge was astonished at the man's clever answers.

'You're not ignorant at all,' he said. 'You deserve your clever wife.'

'Oh,' the ignorant man said proudly. 'It was my wife who gave me the answers.'

'You see?' the clever man said. 'She's too good for this stupid fellow. Give her to me.'

'I agree,' the judge said. 'This fellow is very stupid, after all, and such an intelligent woman should be married to a clever man. She ought to be yours. Go home, my poor ignorant neighbour. Get ready to divorce your wife. And you, sir, make preparations for your wedding.'

The ignorant man went home in great distress.

'My dear wife,' he said. 'I've lost you, and my life is ruined.'

'Did you answer as I told you to?' asked his wife.

'Yes,' the man said. 'But they still want to take you from me.'

'Don't despair,' said his wife. 'Ask the judge and the clever man to come to our house so that I can cook them a meal.'

'I don't see what good that will do,' her husband said, but he did as she asked, and invited the clever man and the judge to his house.

The woman spent the next day preparing a meal, and in the evening it was ready. The guests arrived and she brought them water to wash their hands. Then she fetched the plates of food.

The judge picked up the bread she offered him.

'What's this?' he said.

'It's bread,' the woman answered.

'But it's all black and burned,' said the judge.

The woman offered the clever man the stew pot.

'What kind of stew is this?' he said.

'It's chicken stew,' she said.

He lifted the lid off the pot.

'But you haven't taken the feathers off it!' he said.

'Take this horrible food away,' the judge said to the ignorant man,

'and keep your wife. She's not so clever after all.'

The woman smiled to herself as the judge and the clever man went away. She threw the burnt bread and the chicken stew away.

'Husband, your supper's ready,' she said, bringing out the delicious meal she had prepared for him.

The man and his wife never heard from their clever neighbour again, and they lived together happily for the rest of their lives.

Everything Changes, Everything Passes

 Once there was a merchant, who travelled far and wide through all the land of Ethiopia, selling his wares.

One day, as he was going along the road, he saw a crowd of people.

What are they doing? he thought. What are they looking at? And he hurried over to join them.

The people were watching a farmer who was ploughing his field, but yoked to the plough in the place of an ox there was a man.

The farmer was whipping him cruelly.

'Go on, go on, you lazy good for nothing,' he was shouting. 'Pull harder!'

The merchant was sad when he saw this pitiful sight, and tears began to fall from his eyes. The man pulling the plough looked up and saw his distress.

'Don't cry for me,' he said. 'Don't stop your journey for me.'

The merchant was impressed by the man's courage and dignity.

'This is wrong, this is cruel,' he said, 'that one man should put another man under a yoke as if he was an ox.'

But the man said, 'Listen, my friend. Everything changes, everything passes, and my suffering will pass too.'

So the merchant, shaking his head sadly, went on his way.

A few years later, his travels took him to the very same place again, and he remembered the strange sight he'd seen before.

He stopped a passer-by and said to her, 'A few years ago, in this very place, I saw a man pulling a plough like an ox. What's happened to him? Can he still be alive?'

The woman laughed.

'No,' she said. 'He didn't die. God looked down on him and took pity on his misery. He gave him riches and honour and that very same man is now the king of the whole region.'

The merchant could hardly believe his ears.

'What?' he said. 'In such a short time he has risen from being a slave to being a king?'

'Yes,' the woman said. 'If you don't believe me, go and see him for yourself.'

So the merchant hurried to the king's palace and slipped in through the gate. The man he remembered, dressed in fine clothes, was sitting in state, surrounded by crowds of people. The merchant was so happy

for him he laughed out loud.

The king heard him laugh and called out to him, 'Who are you, stranger? Why are you laughing?'

'Well, sir,' the merchant said, 'as I travelled through this place a few years ago, I saw you pulling a plough like an ox and I wept for you.

I was on the same road today and I heard that you had become king so I came here to see you with my own eyes and to rejoice in your happiness.'

The king smiled.

'Come,' he said, 'and sit beside me. Let's eat and drink,' and he shared his meal with the merchant and gave him gifts as well.

When they had finished eating, the king said, 'My son, God will bless you for remembering the poor man under the yoke.'

'How could I forget you!' the merchant cried. 'And to see you now like this! It's marvellous! Wonderful!'

'Yes,' said the king, 'but everything changes, everything passes, and this happiness of mine will pass too.'

The merchant went on his way, but when a few more years had passed, he returned once more, and hurried straight to the palace of the king to see how his friend was faring. He ran in through the gates, but there, seated in state, was another king, a man he had never seen before.

'Who is this?' he said to the people around him. 'What happened to your king?'

'The old king died,' they told him. 'This man is king now.'

The merchant bowed his head and wept.

'Show me his grave,' he said, 'so that I can pay him my respects.'

So the people took him to the graveyard and showed him the stone under which the king was buried. Sweet grasses blew in the wind and trees shaded his grave. Words were carved on the tombstone and the merchant spelled them out.

'Everything changes, everything passes,' the inscription said. 'And even this will pass too.'

Sadly, the merchant went on his way.

Many years later, when he came again, he hurried eagerly to the graveyard.

Whatever else has happened, the king's grave will still be there, he thought. That cannot change. That cannot pass.

But a modern city had grown up in the meantime and the graveyard had disappeared. The grass, the shady trees, and the tombstones had all disappeared. Workmen were carrying bricks and panes of glass and trucks were spilling out tons of sand and cement.

The merchant called to a workman and said, 'Please, my friend, there was a graveyard here once, and on one of the headstones there was an inscription which read, "Everything changes, everything passes, and even this will pass too." Do you know where it has gone?'

'I remember that stone,' the man said, 'but you won't find it now. The city's master plan has swept the graveyard and all the headstones away, and in its place is that great building. Look.'

The merchant looked up to where the man was pointing and saw a modern building, gleaming with glass and new concrete. He shook his head.

'My friend was right,' he said. 'Everything changes, everything passes, and one day even this great building will disappear too.'

About these stories

Our favourite stories, *Cinderella*, *The Sleeping Beauty*, and *Little Red Riding Hood*, didn't begin their lives in books. They were told in the dark forests of ancient Europe by adults to adults, and if the children happened to be listening that was lucky for them.

Our traditional tales exist only in books now, but in Ethiopia great treasuries of stories still live in people's heads and have never been written down. Old people sit together in the evenings, when the day's work is done, and tell each other tales that were already old hundreds of years ago: inspiring stories full of brave warriors and hunters, clever stories of cunning and trickery, moral tales of love and goodness, funny stories with a rude twist to them, stories about ogres and kings and merchants and farmers and animals, and stories about what happened when the world began.

I went to Ethiopia to find some of these stories, travelling thousands of miles through the high, cool, central Highlands, where people have been Christian since the earliest times, to the hot deserts of the Muslim east, and the warm, humid south and west where older religions still exist alongside Islam and Christianity. The different faiths and cultures of Ethiopia are reflected in the stories, with their contrasting ideas of God and heaven and the spiritual world.

It's not only religions that differ in Ethiopia. It's an incredibly diverse country in other ways as well. The storytellers I met spoke in many different languages and lived in different kinds of houses, some in roomy, round, thatched huts, some in

94

square yellow-stoned houses, some in tin-roofed mud houses, some in the country, some in the town.

One storyteller was shivering with malaria as she told me her tale. Another was peeling mangoes that he'd just plucked from his own tree, while a third broke off his story from time to time to watch the monkeys chattering and quarrelling in the branches overhead. Mohammed Ahmed, who lives on the edge of the hot, dry, desert region of the north-east, took me to the camel market near his house. In the rainy season, Ogota Agiw, who lives in the far south-west of Ethiopia, has to warn his children to be careful because crocodiles waddle out of the great Baro River and come right into his compound.

When you read these stories, imagine how they've always been told. Think of those dark African nights, when mothers and fathers sit in their huts, the door closed against the hyenas and leopards that prowl in the darkness outside. They look down into the red glow of the fire and draw the children close under their soft, white shawls. Then the story-telling begins.

Each story starts with the special words:

Teret teret
Ye lam beret.

Which means something like this:

The cow's in the barn
The sheep's in the fold
Come sit by the fire
There's a tale to be told.

Acknowledgements

Many people helped in the making of this book. The most important were the storytellers, who welcomed me in every corner of Ethiopia, and sat with me hour after hour, telling me their wonderful tales.

Here are the storyteller's names:

Lieut. Akwai Gora, Yisihak Aldade, Tito Bangay, Mohammed Kuyu, Rhamsy Shwoll, Ibrahim M.I. Waytu, Mohammed Ahmed Algani, Bonsamo Miesso, Merga Debelo, Abebe Kebede, Worku Alemu, Kassa Alamrew, Mesele Zeleke, Zeritu Kebede

I couldn't have met the storytellers at all if the cultural officers from different regions hadn't introduced me to them, and given me their enthusiastic help.

Here are some of their names:

Alemayehu Gebrehiwot, Atakilti Hagag, Mohammed Ahmed Algani, Ogota Agiw and Merga Debelo.

I couldn't have understood the stories without the talented translators who explained them to me.

Here are their names:

Michael Daniel Ambatchew, Merga Debelo, Mesele Zeleke, Tsehaynesh Gebre Yohannes, Ogota Agiw, Daniel Legesse, and Mohammed Ahmed Algani

And all this only happened because *Michael Sargent*, Director of the British Council in Ethiopia, set up the story collecting project, *Simon Ingram-Hill* organised it, and the *British Council* and *Department for International Development* funded it. *Teklehaimanot* and *Dirije* drove me thousands of miles in the British Council landrover, and *Michael Daniel Ambatchew* did all the difficult liaison work.

I would like to say thank you to all of them.